Theory of Music
Supplementary Exercises

for Trinity Guildhall Theory of Music
examinations from 2007

Grade 3

by Edwin Gray and Naomi Yandell

Published by
Trinity College London
89 Albert Embankment
London SE1 7TP UK

T +44 (0)20 7820 6100
F +44 (0)20 7820 6161
E music@trinityguildhall.co.uk
www.trinityguildhall.co.uk

Printed in England by Halstan & Co. Ltd, Amersham, Bucks.

Grade 3 𝄞 and 𝄢 notes and note values

1 Name the circled notes in the following music:

Handel

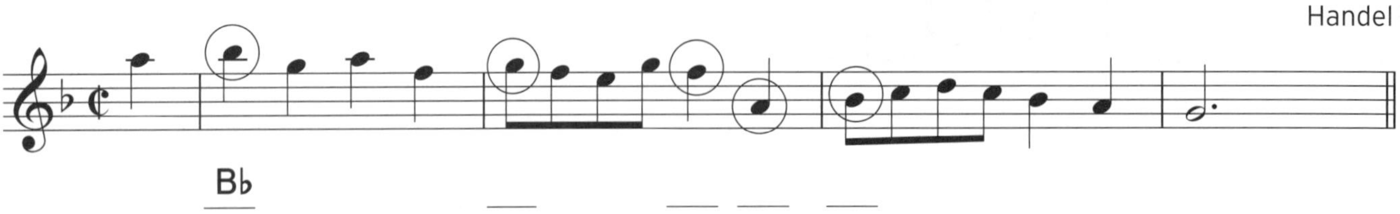

B♭

Beethoven

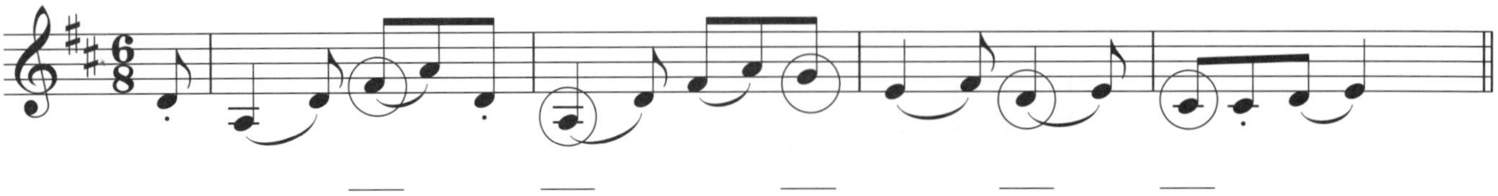

J S Bach

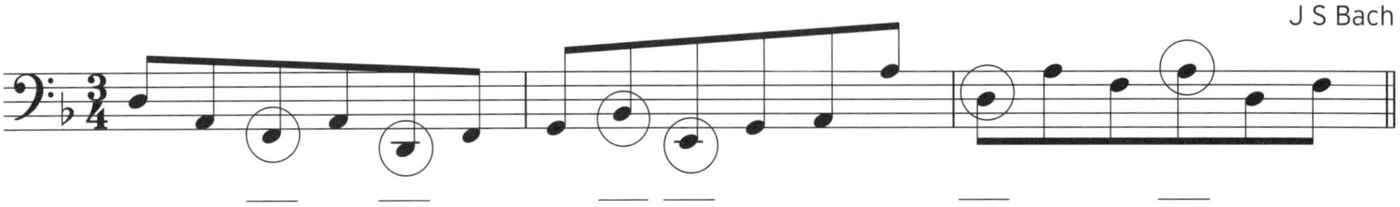

Purcell

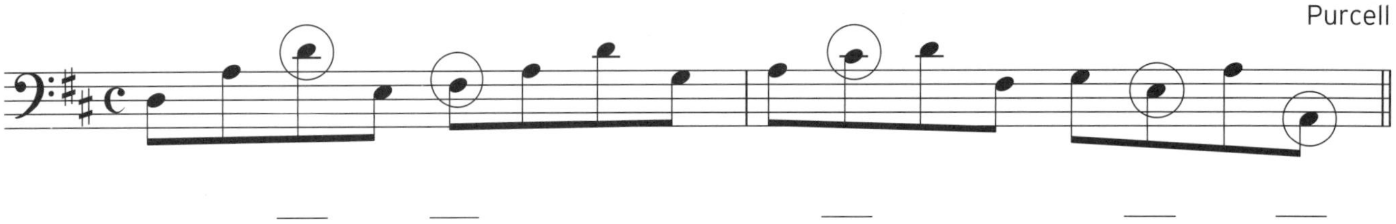

J S Bach

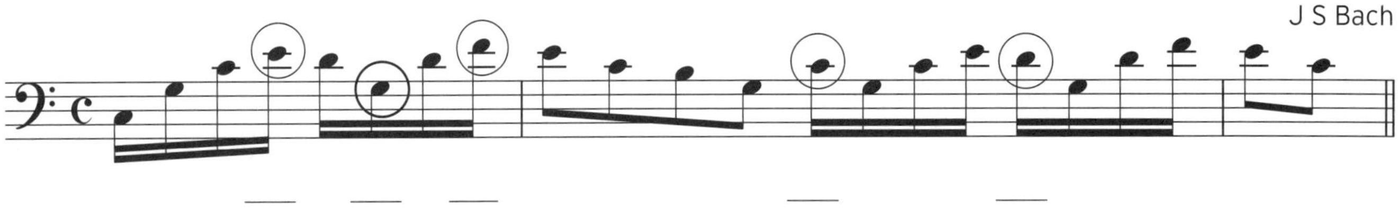

2 Circle five different mistakes in the following music, then write it out correctly.

Example

Andante
mp

Andante
mp

Moderato
mp
3

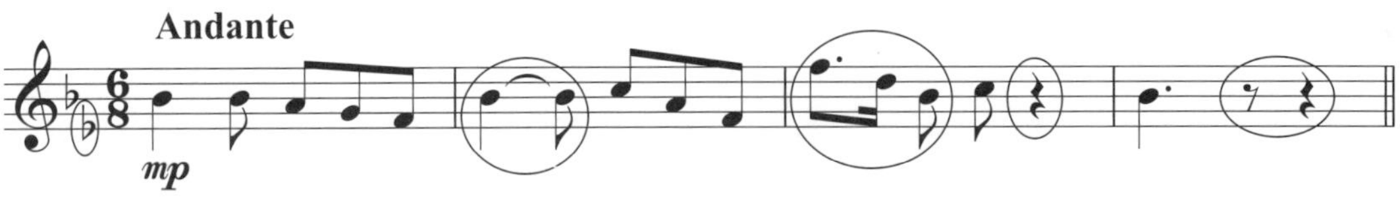

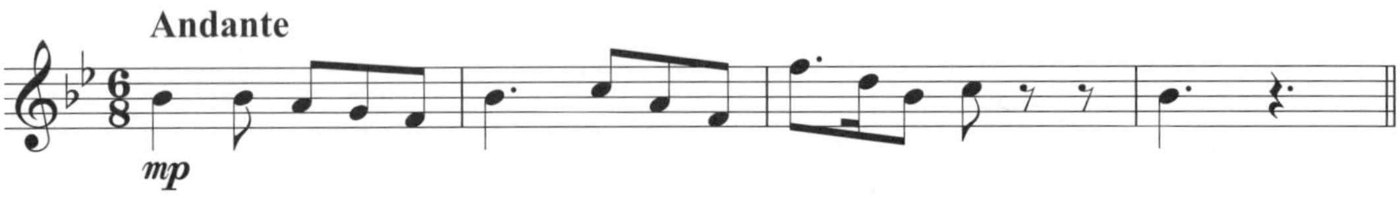

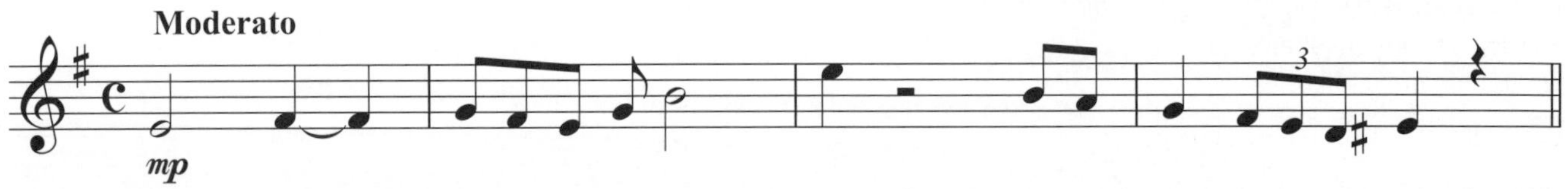

Grouping rests

Add crotchet or quaver rests in the places marked by an asterisk (*) to complete the bars.
Use brackets where necessary.

Grade 3 keys – major and minor scales

1 Write a one-octave B♭ major scale in minims going up then down. Use a key signature.

Example

2 Write a one-octave G melodic minor scale in crotchets going up then down. Use a key signature.

3 Write a one-octave D natural minor scale in semibreves going down then up. Use a key signature.

4 Write a one-octave B harmonic minor scale in crotchets going down then up. Use a key signature.

5 Write a one-octave D major scale in minims going up then down. Use a key signature.

6 Write a one-octave E melodic minor scale in semibreves going down then up. Use a key signature.

7 Write a one-octave F major scale in crotchets going down then up. Use a key signature.

8 Write a one-octave A harmonic minor scale in minims going up then down. Use a key signature.

9 Write a one-octave G major scale in minims going down then up. Do not use a key signature but write in the necessary accidentals.

Example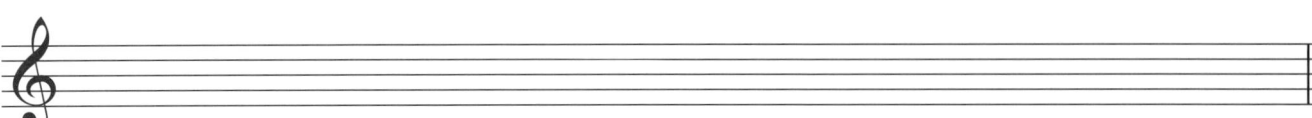

10 Write a one-octave E natural minor scale in crotchets going up then down. Do not use a key signature but write in the necessary accidentals.

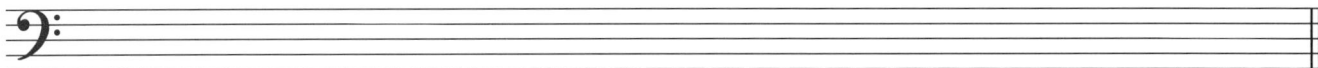

11 Write a one-octave D harmonic minor scale in minims going down then up. Do not use a key signature but write in the necessary accidentals.

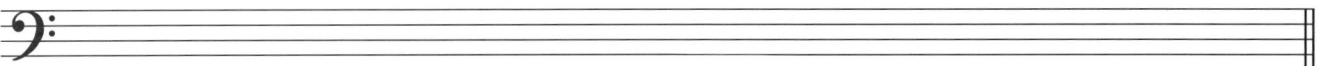

12 Write a one-octave Bb major scale in semibreves going down then up. Do not use a key signature but write in the necessary accidentals.

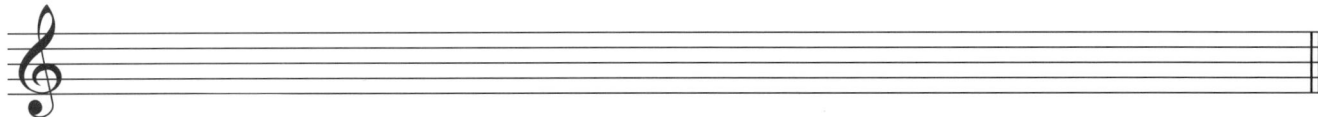

13 Write a one-octave B natural minor scale in crotchets going up then down. Do not use a key signature but write in the necessary accidentals.

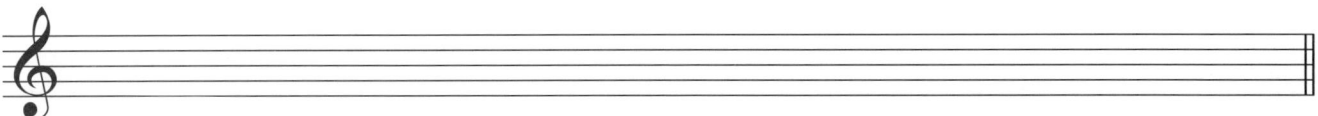

14 Write a one-octave D melodic minor scale in minims going down then up. Do not use a key signature but write in the necessary accidentals.

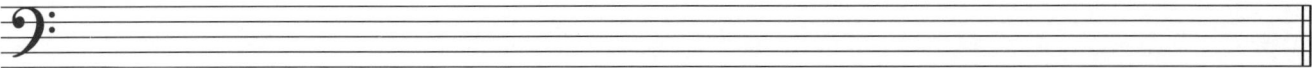

15 Write a one-octave E harmonic minor scale in semibreves going up then down. Do not use a key signature but write in the necessary accidentals.

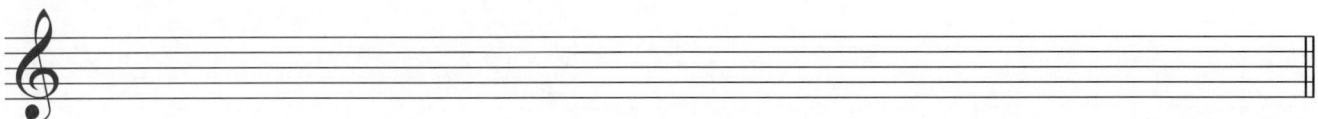

16 Write a one-octave A melodic minor scale in minims going down then up. Do not use a key signature but write in the necessary accidentals.

Key signatures and tonic triad inversions

1 Write the key signature and tonic triad in root and first inversion for each key shown.
Then write its second inversion.

Example

G major   Tonic triad in root position   Tonic triad in first inversion   Tonic triad in second inversion

A minor   Tonic triad in root position   Tonic triad in first inversion   Tonic triad in second inversion

Bb major   Tonic triad in root position   Tonic triad in first inversion   Tonic triad in second inversion

D minor   Tonic triad in root position   Tonic triad in first inversion   Tonic triad in second inversion

F major   Tonic triad in root position   Tonic triad in first inversion   Tonic triad in second inversion

G minor   Tonic triad in root position   Tonic triad in first inversion   Tonic triad in second inversion

C major   Tonic triad in root position   Tonic triad in first inversion   Tonic triad in second inversion

B minor   Tonic triad in root position   Tonic triad in first inversion   Tonic triad in second inversion

E minor   Tonic triad in root position   Tonic triad in first inversion   Tonic triad in second inversion

Arpeggios

1 Write the key signature for each key shown. Then write its one-octave arpeggio in the rhythm given below.

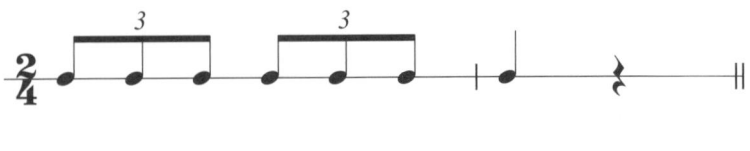

Example

Bb major going up then down

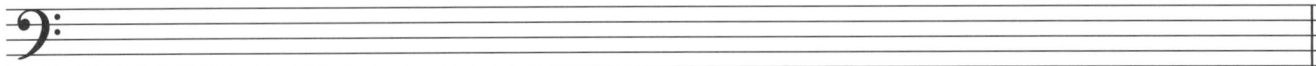

E minor going down then up

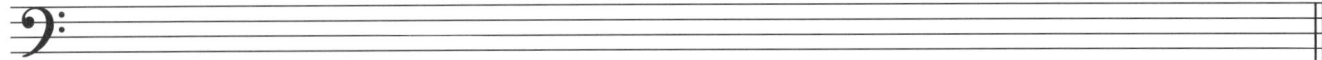

G major going up then down

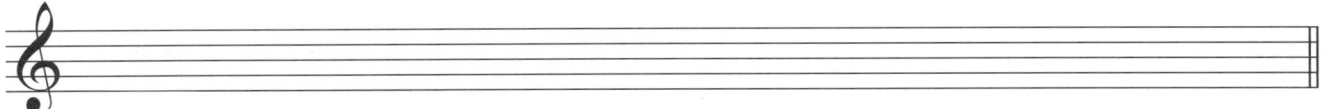

C major going up then down

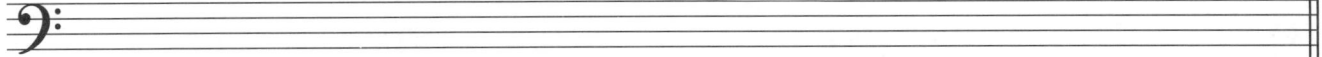

B minor going down then up

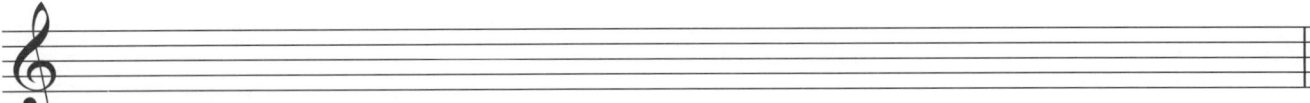

D major going up then down

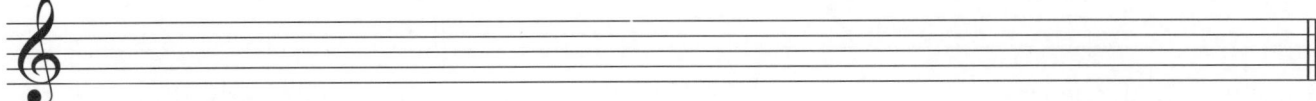

G minor going down then up

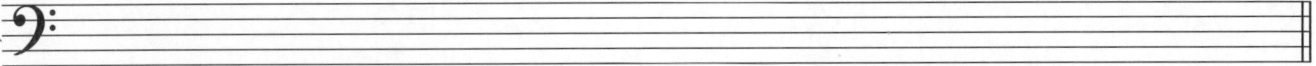

Bb major going down then up

Broken chords

1 Using minims, write a broken chord using B♭ major tonic triad (going up).
Use patterns of three notes each time. Finish on the first **B♭** above the stave.

Example

2 Using quavers, write a broken chord using E minor tonic triad (going up).
Use patterns of four notes each time. Finish on the first **E** above the stave.

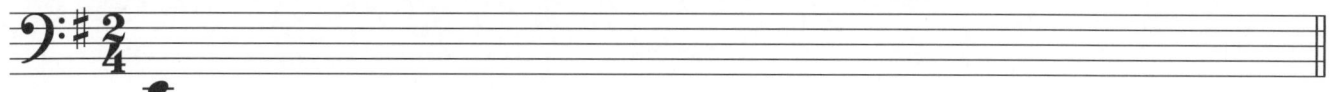

3 Using triplet quavers, write a broken chord using G minor tonic triad (going up).
Use patterns of three notes each time. Finish on the first **B♭** above the stave.

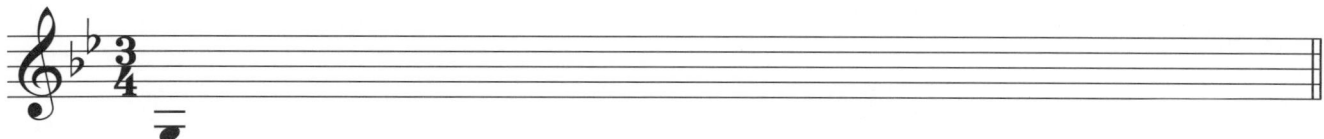

4 Using minims, write a broken chord using D major tonic triad (going down).
Use patterns of three notes each time. Finish on the first **D** below the stave.

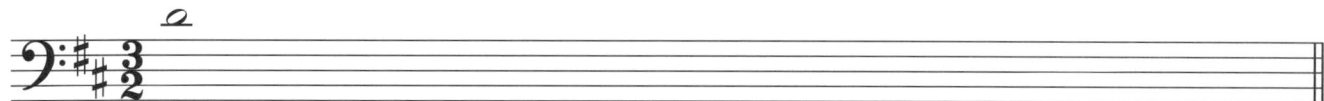

5 Using crotchets, write a broken chord using B minor tonic triad (going up).
Use patterns of three notes each time. Finish on the first **B** above the stave.

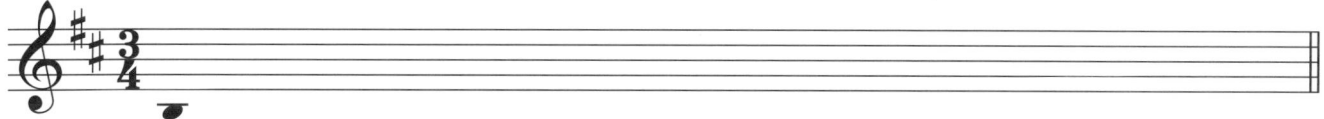

6 Using quavers, write a broken chord using F major tonic triad (going up).
Use patterns of four notes each time. Finish on the **F** on the fifth line of the stave.

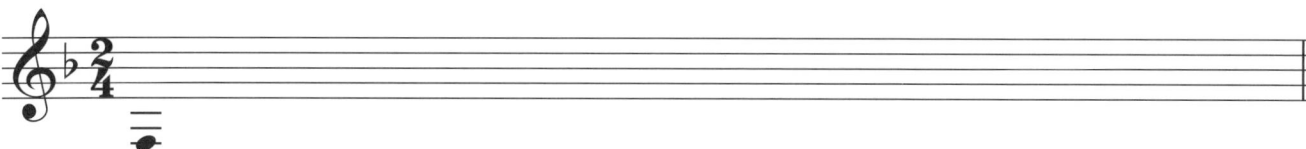

7 Using minims, write a broken chord using D minor tonic triad (going up).
Use patterns of three notes each time. Finish on the first **D** above the stave.

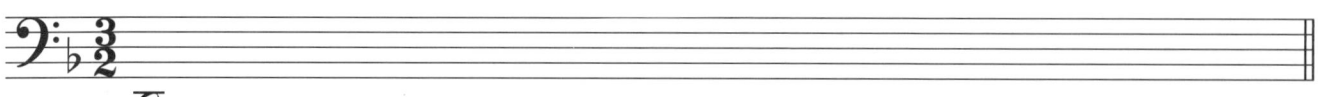

Intervals

Name the following intervals.

Example

Interval: __Major 3rd__

Interval: _____

Interval: _____

Interval: _____

Interval: _____

Interval: _____

Interval: _____

Interval: _____

Real and tonal sequences

Write a bracket (⌐─┐ or └─┘) to show the sequence. Then label it real or tonal.

Triads in major and minor keys

Here are some major and minor scales. Write triads on the tonic and dominant degrees of the scale and label them with Roman numerals below the stave and chord symbols above.

Example

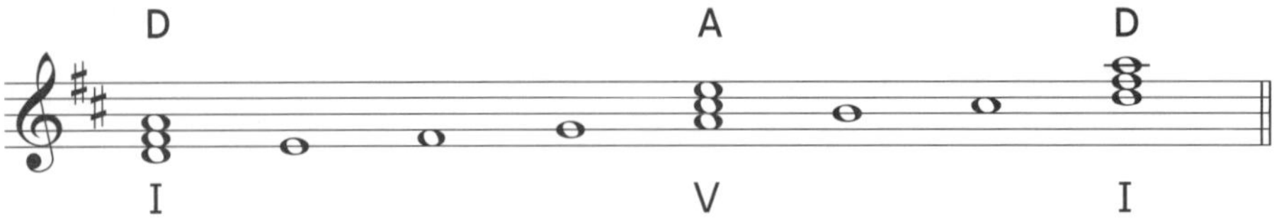

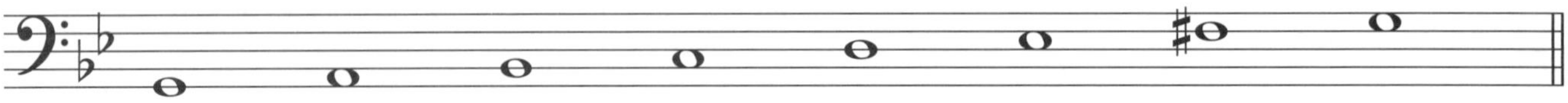

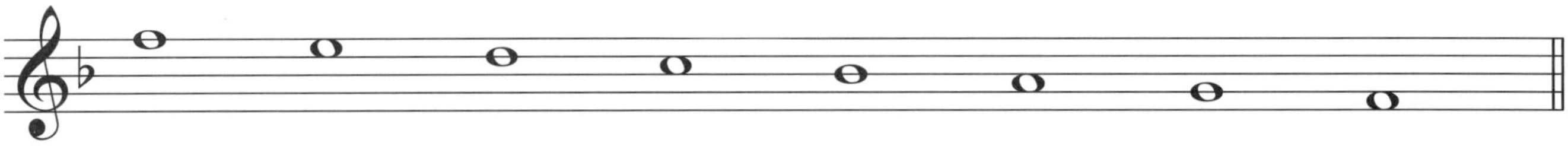

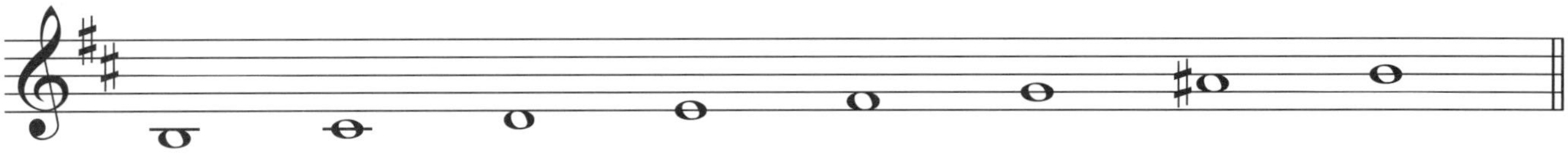

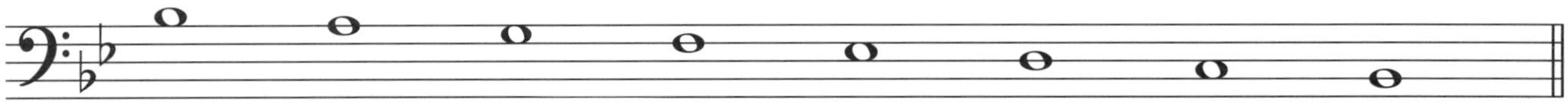

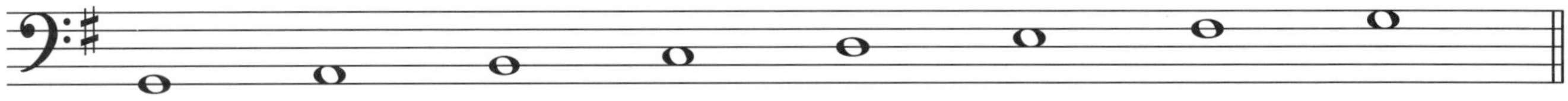

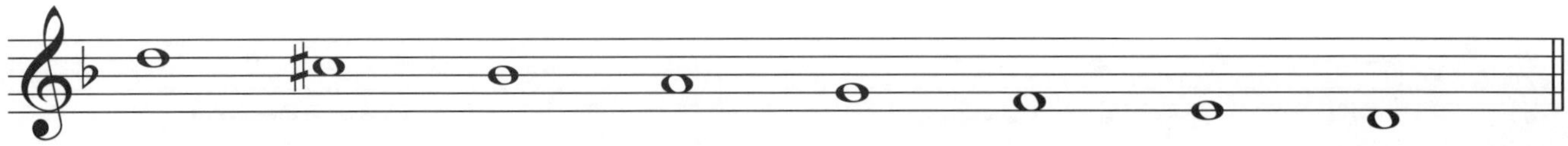

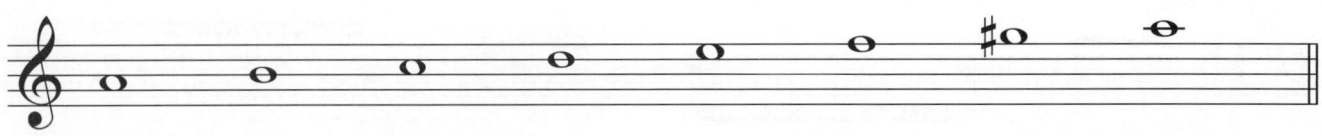

Writing a bass line

1 Use the root of each triad shown by the Roman numerals to write a bass line.

Example

(F major) I I V I

(B♭ major) I V V I

(D major) I I V I

(G minor) i V V i

(B minor) i V V i

2 Use the root of each triad shown by the chord symbols to write a bass line.

Writing a tune

1 Use notes from the tonic or dominant triads shown by the Roman numerals to write a tune above the bass line.

2 Use notes from the tonic or dominant triads shown by the chord symbols to write a tune above the bass line.

4-part chords

Using minims, write out 4-part chords for SATB using the chords shown by the Roman numerals.
Double the root in each case and make sure that each chord is in root position.

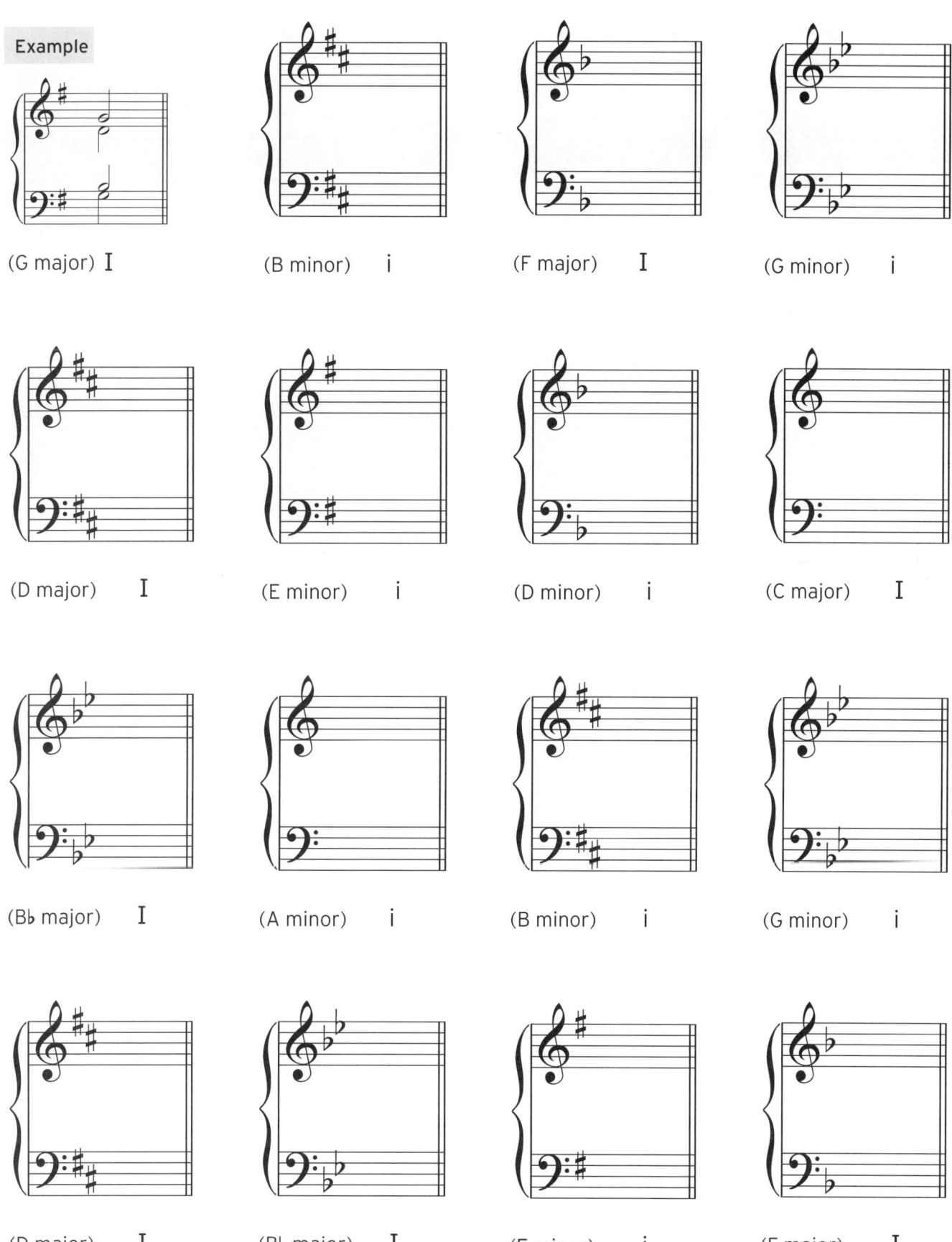

Example

(G major) I

(B minor) i

(F major) I

(G minor) i

(D major) I

(E minor) i

(D minor) i

(C major) I

(B♭ major) I

(A minor) i

(B minor) i

(G minor) i

(D major) I

(B♭ major) I

(E minor) i

(F major) I

Transposing tunes up or down an octave 𝄞 – 𝄢 or 𝄢 – 𝄞

1 Transpose the following tunes down an octave into the bass clef to make them suitable for a cello or bassoon to play.

Traditional (German)

Example

Traditional (American)

Traditional (English)

Traditional (English)

Traditional (French)

18

2 Transpose the following tunes up an octave into the treble clef to make them suitable for a violin or flute to play.

Hopkins

Traditional (German)

Traditional (Scottish)

Traditional (Irish)

Traditional (Polish)

Analysis

1 Look at the following piece and answer the questions on the opposite page.

Traditional (German)

1. In which key is this piece? _____

2. What is the tonic note in this piece? _____

3. Put a bracket (⌐⌐) above three beats where the music moves in similar motion (treble part).

4. Does this piece start on an up-beat or down-beat?_____

5. Write a Roman numeral below the chord in bar 8 to show that the tonic chord accompanies the tune here.

6. What does **Allegretto** mean?_____

7. Is the sequence in bars 13–16 real or tonal (treble part)? _____

8. What does **meno mosso** in bar 9 mean? _____

9. Where is there an instruction to get louder? _____

10. Name the interval between the two notes marked with asterisks (*) in bar 9._____

2 Look at the following piece and answer the questions on the opposite page.

1. In which key is this piece? _____

2. What is the dominant note in this piece? _____

3. Comment on the treble part in bars 1–2 (articulation). _____

4. At what tempo should this piece be played? _____

5. Write a Roman numeral below the second crotchet beat of bar 7 to show that the dominant chord accompanies the tune here.

6. Write a Roman numeral below the first crotchet beat of bar 8 to show that the tonic chord accompanies the tune here.

7. Name the cadence that ends this piece. _____

8. What does **a tempo** in bar 13 mean? _____

9. Is the sequence in bars 9–12 real or tonal (treble part)?_____

10. Name the interval between the two notes marked with asterisks (*) in bar 15. _____

Theory of Music Supplementary Exercises for Trinity Guildhall examinations

This series of supplementary theory exercises has been designed to be used by teachers and students alongside the Trinity Guildhall Theory of Music Workbooks. It has grown out of a demand for extra material to complement the existing workbooks, but it is not intended to replace them.

Trinity Guildhall does not advise entering for a Theory of Music examination without first working through the Trinity Guildhall Theory of Music Workbooks.

The following Trinity Guildhall theory publications are available from your local music shop:

Theory of Music Workbooks for Trinity Guildhall examinations:

Grade 1	TG 006509	ISBN 978-0-85736-000-7
Grade 2	TG 006516	ISBN 978-0-85736-001-4
Grade 3	TG 006523	ISBN 978-0-85736-002-1
Grade 4	TG 006530	ISBN 978-0-85736-003-8
Grade 5	TG 006547	ISBN 978-0-85736-004-5
Grade 6	TG 007476	ISBN 978-0-85736-005-2
Grade 7	TG 007483	ISBN 978-0-85736-006-9
Grade 8	TG 007490	ISBN 978-0-85736-007-6

Theory of Music Supplementary Exercises for Trinity Guildhall examinations:

Grade 1	TG 008787	ISBN 978-0-85736-120-2
Grade 2	TG 008794	ISBN 978-0-85736-121-9
Grade 3	TG 008800	ISBN 978-0-85736-122-6
Grade 4	TG 008817	ISBN 978-0-85736-123-3
Grade 5	TG 008824	ISBN 978-0-85736-124-0

Sample papers for Trinity Guildhall Theory of Music examinations:

Grade 1	TG 006813
Grade 2	TG 006820
Grade 3	TG 006837
Grade 4	TG 006844
Grade 5	TG 006851
Grade 6	TG 007520
Grade 7	TG 007537
Grade 8	TG 007544

Past papers for several years of Theory of Music examinations are also available.

All syllabuses and further information about Trinity Guildhall can be obtained from:

Trinity Guildhall
89 Albert Embankment
London SE1 7TP UK

T +44 (0)20 7820 6100
F +44 (0)20 7820 6161

E music@trinityguildhall.co.uk
www.trinityguildhall.co.uk/music

Trinity Guildhall examinations are offered by Trinity College London, the international examinations board

TG 008800
ISBN 978-0-85736-122-6

9 780857 361226